for Irene

Designed by Louise Millar
Printed and bound in Belgium by Proost
for the publishers Piccadilly Press Ltd.,
5 Castle Road, London NW1 8PR

ISBN: 1 85340 622 8 (paperback)
1 85340 627 9 (hardback)

3 5 7 9 10 8 6 4 2

A catalogue record of this book
is available from the British Library

Rachel Pank lives in London with her husband, two sons and cat.
She has written and illustrated a number of picture books.
This is her first book for Piccadilly.

Rosie's Holiday

Rachel Pank

Piccadilly Press • London

"I don't **want** to go on holiday!"
said a very small girl in a very loud voice.

It was Rosie.

"I like my own room."

"I like my own garden."

"And . . . I like you **all**!" she bellowed
to the cats next door.

The following day, Dad packed the car,
but there wasn't room for everything.
Rosie could not take *all* her cuddly toys.

"Just **one**!" said Dad.

Her bike would not fit, or her duvet,
or the cats next door.

"**No!**" said Dad.
"We'll have to leave
those behind."

So Rosie hugged the cats.
"I will be back!"

She sat in the car wearing her holiday hat,
holding her holiday bag,
and wished she wasn't going.

When they got to their holiday home, Rosie saw the sea, at the bottom of the garden. At first she pretended not to look, but then she saw big blue waves and boats!

Right next door there was a field of cows – with spots! They chewed and smiled at Rosie. "Hello," she said.

Then Rosie followed Mum
and Dad inside.

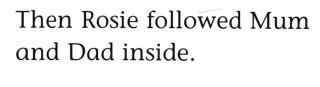

She ran upstairs . . .

. . . and downstairs.

"My holiday bed
is bouncier than
my home bed!"
she shouted.

The next day they all went down to the beach.
Rosie filled her buckets with shells and pebbles.
"I might like it here," she told baby Toby.

Rosie loved the sea.

Every day
she splished . . .

and splashed . . .

and sploshed!

On the last night of the holiday, Rosie stayed up late.
She watched hundreds of twinkling, sparkling stars in
the night sky.
"I **do** like it here," she whispered to her mum and dad.

In the morning, Rosie visited all her favourite places.

"I want to take the
cows home!" she said.

"They like it here," said Dad.
"This is where they belong."
The cows blinked their eyes
and said their goodbyes.

"I want to take the sand
and the sea home,"
Rosie sniffed.

"Look," said Mum. "Here are
your shells and pebbles
to take back. And I've
made you this necklace.
Now we have to pack
and get ready to go."

**"I DON'T WANT TO
GO HOME!"** cried Rosie.

But as soon as they got back to her *very own* home, Rosie raced into the garden.

"You forgot your shells!" called Dad.

But Rosie couldn't wait.

"HELLO!" she shouted to her garden, her paddling pool, the stars and the sky. She hugged her big crocodile and jumped on to her bike.

"It's ME!" she yelled to the cats over the fence . . .

"I'm back!"